Scampa Squirrel's P...

written and illustrated by
Heather S Buchanan

edited by Nina Filipek
designed by Liz Auger

Copyright © 1995 Heather S Buchanan. All rights reserved.
Published in Great Britain by World International,
an imprint of Egmont Publishing Ltd., Egmont House, PO Box 111,
Great Ducie Street, Manchester M60 3BL.
Printed in Finland. ISBN 0 7498 2279 1

A catalogue record for this book is available from the British Library.

N

W — E

S

Basil Bat's
branch

Rumpus Rabbit's
burrow

Muzzy Mouse's
house

Maurice Mole's
hole

Buttercup Meadow stretches from the Deep Dark Wood in the north, where Basil Bat and Scampa Squirrel live, to the small stream in the south, where Maurice Mole has his home.

Henrietta Hedgehog lives in an old log on the east side, and Muzzy Mouse's straw house is under the hedge to the west. In the middle of the meadow lives Rumpus Rabbit.

Scampa Squirrel's tree

Henrietta Hedgehog's log

This is Scampa's story...

Scampa Squirrel lived in a hole half-way up a beautiful beech tree which stood at the edge of the Deep Dark Wood. She loved collecting fruits and seeds in Buttercup Meadow for her foodstore, and she gathered up nuts and acorns from around the woodland trees. But she was always forgetting where she had put them, by the time they were needed. It made her feel cross with herself to be so forgetful.

S campa's friends understood her forgetfulness. Whenever they noticed a little pile of nuts that looked as though they had been forgotten, they carried them along to the squirrel's tree. Maurice Mole sometimes even found them in his tunnels as he burrowed along, because Scampa had buried them, and then couldn't remember where!

One morning, when Maurice found some especially tasty-looking acorns underground, he loaded them into his basket as usual and dragged them into the Deep Dark Wood for Scampa.

S campa lowered her own big basket when she heard the little mole calling up to her.

"Come up and have some tea!" the squirrel called back. Maurice climbed into the basket, leaving the acorns at the foot of the tree, and Scampa pulled on the rope to winch him up. The basket lift had been invented by the mole some while ago to help visitors, who like himself, couldn't quite manage to climb Scampa's tall tree.

Maurice sat beside Scampa on her balcony for a while, admiring the splendid view. He could see his latest trail of earthworks stretching across Buttercup Meadow towards the river, which glinted like glass in the morning sunshine.

"How beautiful it all looks from up here," thought the little mole, as he sipped tea with Scampa on the balcony.

"With all these acorns you found I could make a giant acorn pizza and we could have a party with all our friends," suggested the squirrel. Mole, who loved parties, thought it was a wonderful idea.

After Maurice had reached the ground again he unloaded Scampa's acorns from his basket into hers, ready for Scampa to haul them up. Then he set off as fast as his little legs could carry him to spread the news about the party.

First he ran to the middle of the meadow where he woke Rumpus Rabbit, who was dozing in the sun outside his burrow.

"Come to Scampa's at sunset for a surprise!" he shouted. The rabbit jumped up and looked pleased. He liked things to look forward to, particularly when they were coming soon.

T he mole hurried along to Henrietta Hedgehog's log next. He found her gathering herbs in her garden to put in a tussie-mussie, which is a kind of posy.

"Oh yes, I'll be there," she called. "And I'll bring this tussie-mussie along as a present for Scampa."

It was mid-afternoon by the time Maurice Mole reached the blackberry hedge, far away at the western edge of Buttercup Meadow.

Muzzy Mouse was leaning out of the open door of her little straw house, which was tucked into the hedge, almost hidden by the leaves.

She was very excited. "I'll bring a blackberry pudding," she promised.

As Basil Bat swooped home to his pine tree in the Deep Dark Wood late that afternoon, he passed Scampa, still daydreaming on her balcony about what to wear for the party. She had forgotten all about the acorns in the basket at the foot of the tree. But there was still plenty of time yet before she needed to haul them up to start cooking.

Scampa told Basil about the party and invited him to come. He noticed the splendid collection of acorns in her basket on the ground and his mouth watered in anticipation.

Once the dough was ready on the table, Scampa remembered her acorns, and stepped out on to her balcony to heave them up. But when the basket arrived she was horrified when she looked inside. It was completely empty! She peered down through the branches but she couldn't see any sign of her acorns. She was desperate. It was nearly sunset and all the animals would soon be arriving. She had nothing else to give them!

A little later, when Basil was still circling around in the Deep Dark Wood, he noticed something unusual. A group of young voles were having a bowling match under a pine tree. Ten, fat juicy acorns were lined up in a row, and one, without its acorn cup, was being aimed at the others to knock them over. The voles were squeaking with excitement.

The acorns looked just like the ones the bat had seen in Scampa's basket. Basil swooped down to take a closer look.

The voles were very frightened.
"Where did you get those acorns?"
Basil demanded.

Feeling ashamed because they knew they had stolen them, the voles muttered that they had found them in a basket and thought no one wanted them.

"Well, you can take them straight back," growled Basil.

The voles did so at once, mumbling that they were very sorry indeed.

"**Y**ou've been good little voles to own up," said Scampa, feeling much happier again when she saw her acorns. "Why don't you come to the party, too. There will be plenty of food for everyone!"

Basil went back to tell their parents where they were, whilst they helped Scampa prepare the pizza.

They shredded the acorns with their sharp teeth and added buttercup petals, mixing them together and arranging them on the big piece of dough. Then Scampa put the pizza in the oven. It looked delicious when it was cooked.

The party was a great success. The other animals all brought lanterns and hung them round the trees. First of all they had Scampa's acorn pizza, then Muzzy's enormous blackberry pudding.

After that, when the food had gone, the entertainment began. The voles sang, and then did acrobatics to loud applause.

When it was really dark, all the animals danced, holding paws, in a circle around Henrietta's tussie-mussie till dawn came. Then the tired little voles were collected by their parents and the other animals lay down to sleep in Scampa's house.

The squirrel and the bat dozed together outside on the balcony, watching the sunrise.

"If I hadn't been so forgetful about the acorns, we'd never have met those little voles," she smiled. "And they made it the best party ever!"

Basil was asleep, upside down, so he couldn't reply.

The End

TITLES IN THE BUTTERCUP MEADOW SERIES
BY HEATHER S BUCHANAN

RUMPUS RABBIT
HENRIETTA HEDGEHOG
MAURICE MOLE
SCAMPA SQUIRREL
BASIL BAT
MUZZY MOUSE